Cookie Chaos

'Cookie Chaos'
An original concept by Jenny Moore
© Jenny Moore 2024

Illustrated by Robbie Hardianto

Published by MAVERICK ARTS PUBLISHING LTD
Suite 1, Hillreed House, 54 Queen Street,
Horsham, West Sussex, RH13 5AD
© Maverick Arts Publishing Limited September 2024
+44 (0)1403 256941

A CIP catalogue record for this book is available at the British Library.

ISBN 978-1-83511-032-*

Printed in India

www.maverickbooks.co.uk

Shropshire Libraries	
7700000549002X	
PETERS	16-Oct-2024
	6.99

This book is rated as: Gold Band (Guided Reading)

Cookie Chaos

By Jenny Moore

Illustrated by Robbie Hardianto

Chapter 1

Mattie was getting everything sorted for Grandma's big surprise party. She pulled a strand of seaweed from her hair, and checked her to-do list.

She and Dad had mopped the floor, dusted the shelves and polished the big shell mirror until it gleamed. They'd hung the seaweed streamers and prepared the party food.

The whale music Dad had recorded for Grandma's birthday present was all ready to play. And Mattie had finally finished the big birthday banner she'd been working on all week.

HAPPY BIRTHDAY GRANDMA, it said. **HOPE YOU HAVE A WHALE OF A TIME.**

She'd even added a pinch of her mum's magic shell powder to the paint mix. It made the whales look like they were swimming!

All that was missing now were the guests— and Grandma of course! Mum had taken her out for the day so Mattie and Dad could get things ready.

Dad had popped out to pick up Grandma's old school friend Coral, and the other guests would be arriving soon.

"That's everything on the list," Mattie told her pet lobster, Lollo. "I think we're ready."

Lollo tipped his head on one side, snapped his claws and spun around in a circle. That's what he *always* did when he was excited.

"I'm excited too," said Mattie. "I can't wait to see the look of surprise on Grandma's face! She's going to love the whale music, and the special whale cookies I made." Mattie gasped. "Oh no, the cookies! I still need to ice them!"

Chapter 2

"We'll have to hurry," Mattie told Lollo, grabbing a mixing bowl. "Can you pass me the icing sugar? It's just behind you. Thanks," she said, tipping the whole jar in without looking.

She added a squirt of blue squid ink and a few vanilla drops, then mixed it all together. The finished icing was a little runny but it would have to do.

"There," said Mattie when she'd finished. "We did it, Lollo! Fourteen iced blue whales and one left over! There's not enough icing left for him, so I'll pop him in the biscuit tin for tomorrow."

She stepped back to admire her work. The iced whales looked great. The sticky blue splashes all over the worktop didn't look quite so good though.

"I'll put these on the table with the rest of the food and then come back and tidy up," she said.

Mattie washed up the mixing bowl and wiped up the spills and splashes so everything would be nice and clean for Grandma's big surprise. But Mattie was the one who was surprised when she picked up the empty icing sugar jar... and it wasn't a *good* surprise.

"Oh no!"

she cried. "This isn't icing sugar! It's Mum's magic shell powder!" Lollo must have passed her the wrong jar by mistake.

Mum sometimes used a tiny pinch of shell powder in her cooking to bring the flavours to life. She'd been happy for Mattie to add a pinch to her paint too, to give the whales on Grandma's birthday banner a bit of magic and movement. She *wouldn't* be happy when she discovered Mattie had used the whole jar to make icing though. And what about the cookies? What would happen to them?

Just then, a strange clicking, moaning noise came from the other room.

"Uh-oh," said Mattie. "That sounds like a whale. *Lots* of whales."

Chapter 3

Mattie's mouth fell open at the sight of her freshly iced whale cookies swimming off the plate. They weren't cookies anymore though. They were *real* whales, and they were growing bigger with every passing second.

"Oh no, look, Lollo!" she cried.

"Mum's magic shell powder must have brought them to life. I can't give Grandma *these* cookies to eat and there's no time to bake any more. This is a disaster!"

CRASH!

A whale's tail sent a tray of cheese and seaweed rolls flying across the room.

CLATTER!

A whale fin brushed against the cutlery holder, sending knives and forks everywhere.

SMASH! A big plate of sea lettuce sandwiches broke into pieces as it hit the floor.

Mattie stared at the mess in horror. Two of the whales were tangled in the seaweed streamers.

RIP! They tore through the streamers as they twisted themselves free, bringing the birthday banner down with them.

"No!" cried Mattie. "Stop! Stay still! Don't get any bigger!"

But the whales kept swimming round in circles, knocking things over. They were still growing too. Soon they'd be too big to swim out the door.

"You need to get out of here or you'll get stuck! This way! Quickly!" cried Mattie.

The cave wasn't big enough for *one* fully grown blue whale, let alone fourteen!

Chapter 4

It took a while, but at last the final whale squeezed through the door and swam away.

"Phew!" said Mattie, as she watched it go. "We got them out just in time."

But then she turned round and saw the terrible mess they'd left behind.
Her heart sank.

"It's too late to save the party, though. Look, Lollo, they even broke the music player. That means we've got no party food, no decorations and no special whale music to play for Grandma. It's going to be the worst birthday party ever." She burst into tears.

Mattie was still crying when Dad arrived with Grandma's old school friend, Coral. Dad stared around the cave in shock. "What happened here? Are you okay?"

Mattie nodded. "I'm sorry," she said. "I put magic powder in the icing by mistake and my whale cookies turned into *real* whales.

They broke everything. I've ruined Grandma's party."

Dad put his arms round her. "It's okay. Don't cry. I'll help you tidy up before she gets here."

"I'll help too," said Coral. "I'll whip up some party pancakes to replace the lost food. And look, here come the other guests. If we all work together as a team, we can still save the party."

Everyone was happy to help. Soon the cave was full of family and friends all working together. Some were in the kitchen with Coral, making big stacks of party pancakes.

Others were clearing up the mess in the main room, tidying and sweeping and rehanging the torn banner.

They didn't have long though.

"Quick!" called Mattie, spotting Mum and Grandma through the window. "Here she comes! Take your places everyone."

Chapter 5

"SURPRISE!" everybody shouted as Grandma swam through the door. **"HAPPY BIRTHDAY!"**

"Oh my!" said Grandma. "This *is* a surprise! How lovely!"

"There were more decorations than this before," Mattie explained. "And more food. Dad even recorded some special whale music for you too. But I had a bit of a mix-up with the icing sugar when I was finishing your whale cookies…"

She told Grandma what had happened. Her eyes filled with tears again at the thought of all that hard work going to waste.

Grandma hugged her tight. "What a shame," she said. "Your cookies sound lovely. But don't feel bad, Mattie. Having all my friends and family together is the nicest present I could ask for. And I can't wait to tuck into these pancakes."

"Wait! I've just remembered," said Mattie. "There's one cookie left in the biscuit tin."

She fetched the spare cookie and gave it to Grandma.

"It's not iced, I'm afraid. And you'll have to imagine all its friends," she added with a wink.

"No you won't," said Mum, pointing out the window. "Look!"

Everyone watched in wonder as fourteen blue whales swam slowly back past the cave, filling the sea with their song.

"Oh my!" said Grandma. "That was beautiful. This is the best birthday *ever*."

The End

Book Bands for Guided Reading

The Institute of Education book banding system is a scale of colours that reflects the various levels of reading difficulty. The bands are assigned by taking into account the content, the language style, the layout and phonics. Word, phrase and sentence level work is also taken into consideration.

Maverick Early Readers are a bright, attractive range of books covering the pink to white bands. All of these books have been book banded for guided reading to the industry standard and edited by a leading educational consultant.

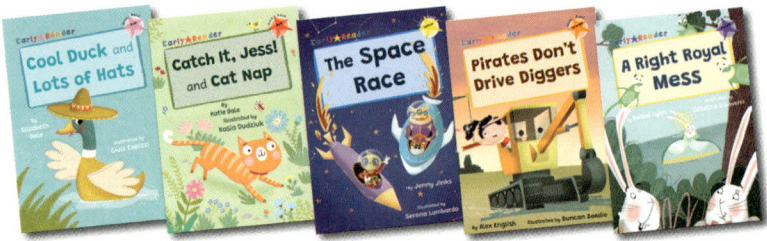

To view the whole Maverick Readers scheme, visit our website at www.maverickearlyreaders.com

Or scan the QR code above to view our scheme instantly!